GREAT ILLUSTRATED CLASSICS

THE
TIME MACHINE

H.G. Wells

adapted by
Shirley Bogart

Illustrations by
Brendan Lynch

BARONET
BOOKS

BARONET BOOKS, New York, New York

GREAT ILLUSTRATED CLASSICS

edited by
Malvina G. Vogel

Contents

CHAPTER   PAGE

1. A Strange Disappearance 7
2. A Late Arrival 25
3. The Time Traveler's Story 37
4. Landing in the Year 802,701 A.D....... 49
5. Strange Little People 67
6. The Time Machine Vanishes 85
7. Weena of the Eloi 103
8. Down to the "Bad Place" 121
9. A Terrible Truth! 135
10. Trapped by the Morlocks 153
11. The Time Machine Is Found 171
12. Escape to the Future 187
13. The Golden Age of Science 203
14. One Story Ends and
    Another Begins 229

About the Author

Henry George Wells did not appear to have much chance for success in life. Born in 1866 in Bromley, Kent, England, to a rather poor family, he was not given a very good early education.

To give him a chance to earn a modest living, his parents apprenticed him first to a cloth maker and then to a pharmacist. But the boy found both jobs boring and ran away.

Young Wells had always read a lot on his own, and he was able to get a job as a teacher's aide. At this point, he was encouraged to take a special exam, and he won a scholarship to the Royal College of Science, where he studied biology. In 1888, Wells graduated with first-class honors from the University of London.

H. G. Wells had always been interested in science fiction, and when he began writing it himself, he tried to include in some of his works his political ideas for the perfect society of the future. In *The Time Machine,* Wells's Time Traveler seeks that ideal civilization.

Besides this, Wells added other imaginative touches which, in 1895, were unheard of. For example, the idea of *time* as the fourth dimension after length, width, and depth was not discussed or accepted in the scientific world until 1905, when Albert Einstein published his paper on the relativity of time.

Even more startling, in *A World Set Free* in 1914, Wells described atomic bombs. These were not used until World War II in 1945.

H. G. Wells died in 1946, leaving behind such successful non-fiction works as *The Outline of History* and *The Science of Life.* But it was through his great science fiction works and the movies made from them that H. G. Wells will always be best remembered: *The Time Machine, The Island of Dr. Moreau, The Invisible Man,* and *The War of the Worlds.*

"What Has Happened to You?"

CHAPTER 1

A Strange Disappearance

"Good Heavens, man!" gasped Filby. "What has happened to you?"

Standing in the doorway to his dining room, bruised and disheveled, the young scientist wore the look of one who had just been through unspeakable horror. He just stood there, silently shaking his head.

The other men seated around the table echoed Filby's amazement at the appearance of their host, a respected young scientist.

As all the guests stared, frozen in their chairs, Filby's mind raced back to the strange events of the week before.

THE TIME MACHINE

That evening, as the scientist's dinner guests were all sitting around the table after one of his regular Thursday dinner parties at his stately home in Richmond, England, the host had captured everyone's attention with a point he was making. To avoid using the scientist's name, let him just be known as the Time Traveler.

Among the invited guests were George Filby, a mathematics professor and the Time Traveler's closest friend; John Manning, a psychologist; and Oswald Perry, a doctor.

The men had been discussing the educational system in England when the Time Traveler burst out, "And another thing — they're not teaching geometry correctly in today's schools."

"What are you talking about?" asked Filby. "We do an excellent job of teaching math."

"I figure that system of math produced fine results with all of us," observed Manning as he

Discussing Education in England

waved his arm to include all the educated men present.

The Time Traveler raised his hand excitedly. "No, no. You must let me explain."

"Go ahead. Tell us what's wrong with the way we learned and are teaching the subject," said Filby, briskly running his fingers through his wiry red hair.

"Okay," said the Time Traveler. "First of all, they taught us that a line can be measured only one way — by how long it is. Right?" And he drew a straight line across his napkin.

"A line has one dimension, its length. You're right so far," said Dr. Perry.

"Now I draw a square," continued the Time Traveler, adding three more lines to turn his diagram into a square. "*Now* how many dimensions does it have?"

"Two, of course," said Manning.

"Everybody knows that," said Filby impatiently. "A flat object has both length and

Two Dimensions—Length and Width

width. Get on with it, man."

"All in good time." The Time Traveler's eyes twinkled, as if at some secret joke. "Now," he continued, holding up his cube-shaped cigar humidor, "how about this cube? How many dimensions does *it* have?"

"Are you putting us on?" cried Perry. "It has *three,* of course — length, width, and thickness. Do I go to the head of the class?" Perry's blue eyes gleamed behind his glasses.

"I'm quite serious," said the Time Traveler. "Length, width, and depth, . . . *and that's all they ever teach you in school!*" His hand slammed the table in anger.

"Hold on now," said Manning. "Are you trying to tell us that there's *more* . . . that there's *another* dimension besides length, width, and depth?"

"There certainly is. Look at this composite portrait of myself, for starters. Three sections, right? First I'm five." He pointed at one

Three Dimensions—Length, Width, and Depth

section. "Next you see me at twelve . . . and finally, here I'm twenty years old. How many dimensions do you see?"

"The same three, of course," said Filby. "The canvas and frame have length, width, and depth."

"Aha!" said the Time Traveler. "And *that's* where you're wrong!"

"Wait a minute," said Manning. "I think I know what you're getting at. Are you talking about *time?*"

"Exactly!" shouted the Time Traveler. "Time — the one factor they always manage to skip in teaching us geometry — *time* is the fourth dimension!"

"But don't you see," said Perry, "the reason they leave it out is quite obvious. Length, width, and depth are dimensions in space. We can move back and forth, and up and down in space. But we can't go backward or forward in time."

"Time is the Fourth Dimension!"

"Wrong, *wrong*, WRONG!" cried the Time Traveler. "The fact is . . . we *can*."

"What do you mean?" asked Filby, getting up. "I am now walking across the room to this door and back. I can go up and down on a staircase or in a balloon. I can move in space, but I can't move into yesterday or tomorrow. None of us can."

"That," said the Time Traveler quietly, "is only your opinion. I have been working on experiments for years, and I can now tell you of my great discovery. It is a machine that is capable of taking us into the past or into the future."

Everyone at the table laughed.

"Impossible!"

"Ridiculous!"

"Absurd!"

"Don't laugh, my friends," said the Time Traveler. "It is not impossible or ridiculous or absurd."

"I Can Move in Space, but . . . . "

"Really? Then how about showing us what you've done," said Manning.

"Yes, let's see your experiment," said Filby, "though I fear it's all a bunch of nonsense."

The Time Traveler smiled at his guests and walked out of the room. They heard his footsteps heading down the long passage to his laboratory.

Perry looked at the other men. "I wonder what it is he's getting?" he asked, puzzled.

"Probably some magician's trick," said Manning.

Filby said nothing, but waited with growing curiosity.

Soon his host returned, holding in his hand something that glittered. It was a metallic framework hardly bigger than a small clock, and very delicately made, with some ivory and some transparent crystalline parts.

The Time Traveler moved a small eight-sided table over to the fireplace and put the

Smiling at His Guests

mechanism on it. A shaded lamp standing on the table threw a bright light on the model.

The Time Traveler looked first at his guests, then at the object. "I would like to explain," he began, "that this is only a *model* of my Time Travel Machine. Notice this twinkling part above this bar, and these two levers."

"It's beautifully made," said Filby.

"It took me about two years to complete," said the Time Traveler. Then, pointing to a kind of saddle, he explained, "This is where the Time Traveler sits, and these . . . " and he pointed to two small bars " . . . these two little white levers control the time. The first one sends the machine gliding into the future, and this other reverses the motion."

All the men got up and gathered around the table for a closer look.

"When do you plan to test it out?" asked Perry.

"In a few seconds. But first, I want you all

The Model of the Time Machine

to examine everything carefully. Check the table too. I don't want to waste this model and then have you tell me I'm a quack, for once the machine leaves, it will vanish into the future and disappear."

"Are you really going to set it off?" asked Manning.

"Yes, I am. No, better yet, you are. Lend me your hand, Manning. This way, you can't say it's a fake."

The Time Traveler directed the psychologist to put out his forefinger and push the lever. Everyone in that room saw the lever move, and everyone was absolutely certain there was no trickery.

Suddenly, a puff of wind from the model made the lamp flame jump. The little machine quickly swung around, blurred, and resembled a faint ghost of itself. Then it vanished completely. Except for the lamp, the table was bare!

Pushing the Lever

"Could It Be Under the Table?"

CHAPTER 2

A Late Arrival

"Well, I'll be darned! " said Filby.

"Could it be under the table?" asked Manning, bending to check.

This made the Time Traveler laugh.

"Come now!" said Dr. Perry. "Do you really believe that your contraption has traveled into *time*?"

"Of course I do," said the Time Traveler. "Otherwise I wouldn't be wasting your time."

Manning was trying hard to show he was not at all upset by the strange disappearance. Coolly, he tried to light his cigar. The trouble was, he'd forgotten to cut off the tip and was having difficulty igniting the uncut end.

"Do you mean to say that your machine has gone into the future?" he asked between hard, smokeless puffs.

"Either the future or the past — I'm not sure which," said the Time Traveler. "You see, it has not moved through space, only through *time*. Since it passed through large portions of time in only a second, its appearance thinned out, and it became invisible."

"It all seems very believable right now," said the doctor, "but I wonder what we'll think about all this tomorrow, when our common sense returns."

"Would you like to see the actual Time Machine itself?" asked the Time Traveler.

Everyone present thought their host must be joking. "What are you saying?" cried Manning.

"You can't be serious!" added Perry.

"What a sense of humor!" said Filby.

Has the Machine Gone into the Future?

"Just follow me," said the Time Traveler. And with the lamp in his hand, he led the way down the long, drafty corridor to his lab.

The men followed, puzzled, and not ready to believe until their host flung open the lab door. There, before their eyes stood a full-sized version of the little mechanism that had vanished in the dining room. Parts of the Time Machine were of nickel, parts were of ivory, and parts had been sawed out of rock crystal.

The thing seemed to be complete, except for the twisted crystalline bars which lay unfinished on the workbench alongside some drawings.

Filby picked up one bar for a better look. "Quartz, isn't it?" he asked.

The Time Traveler smiled and nodded.

"Listen, now," said Filby to the Time Traveler. "Are you really serious? Or is this another trick like the so-called ghost you made appear last Halloween?"

The Full-Sized Time Machine

THE TIME MACHINE

The Time Traveler held the lamp high and pointed dramatically. "In that machine, I intend to explore Time," he said. "Is that clear? I was never more serious about anything in my whole life!"

During the following week, Filby ran into the doctor at their club. "What do you think of what we saw last Thursday?" Filby asked.

"Well, you know our scientist friend has always been a bit of a joker. Clever, yes. But it's hard to take him seriously."

"But how about the way he made that model disappear?"

"It was a good trick, all right," said Dr. Perry with a laugh. "Reminds me of one I saw performed at a magic show. Can't explain either one of them."

"Are you going to dinner with our Time Traveler again this Thursday?" asked Filby.

"I plan to. See you there."

"In That Machine, I Intend To Explore Time."

Filby arrived late for the Time Traveler's dinner party that following Thursday and found four men already gathered in the drawing-room. He recognized Clark, an editor, and Brice, a writer, in addition to Dr. Perry and Manning. But their host was nowhere to be seen.

Perry was standing by the fire with a piece of paper in one hand and his watch in the other. "It's half-past seven," he said. "I guess we'd better go in to dinner."

"Without our host?" asked Filby.

Perry held up the piece of paper and explained, "He left this note for whoever arrived first. He says he might be detained, and to start off without him at seven if he wasn't here. Says he'll explain when he comes."

"It certainly seems a shame," said Editor Clark, who looked as if he didn't skip too many meals.

The doctor rang the dinner bell, and the men

Perry Reads the Time Traveler's Note.

seated themselves around the large oval table.

"Wonder why he's late," said Clark.

"It could be that he's tripping through time," Filby said jokingly.

"What do you mean?" asked Brice, the writer.

"Well, you see," began Manning, "last week he showed us this ingenious trick with a little model of what he called a Time Machine, and ... "

The door from the corridor opened slowly and noiselessly. Filby was facing that way and was the first to notice its movement. "At last!" he cried.

Then the door opened wider, and Filby saw him. "My God!" he shouted.

Dr. Perry, who was the next to see him, stared in wonder.

"Good heavens, man!" gasped Filby. "What has happened to you?"

"What Has Happened to You?"

Haggard and Drawn!

CHAPTER 3

The Time Traveler's Story

Everybody turned toward the door. There stood the Time Traveler, in a terrible state. His dusty coat had a green smear down the sleeves. His hair looked grayer to Filby than he had remembered it, but he couldn't tell if the color had changed or if it was just the effect of dust. The Time Traveler's face looked pale as a ghost's; his chin had a half-healed cut on it, and his whole expression was haggard and drawn, as if he'd undergone some intense suffering.

He hesitated in the doorway for a minute, as though dazzled by the light. Then he slowly and painfully limped into the room and sat down.

Without saying a word, he motioned toward the wine. Clark filled a glass of champagne and pushed it toward him. The Time Traveler gulped it down, and it seemed to do him good, for he looked around the table at his friends, and the ghost of his old, familiar smile flickered across his face.

"What on earth have you been up to, man?" asked the doctor.

"Don't let me disturb you," the Time Traveler said haltingly. He held the glass out for a refill, which he drained. "That's good," he said. His eyes grew brighter, and the color began to return to his cheeks. "I'm going to wash and dress," he said slowly. "Then I'll come down and try to explain what happened .... Save me some of that mutton. I'm starving for a bit of meat."

He put down his glass and walked toward the door that led to the staircase. Again Filby

Clark Fills the Time Traveler's Glass.

noticed his lameness and the soft padding sound of his footsteps. Glancing down, he saw his host's feet as they padded out. There was nothing on them but a pair of tattered socks, and they were blood-stained!

Filby felt like following him to see if he needed help. Then he remembered how his friend hated to have anyone fuss over him, so he forced himself to return his attention to the dinner table.

"What's up?" asked Brice. "Has he been playing the amateur beggar? I don't get it."

"I have a feeling it's got something to do with the Time Machine," said Filby, and he went on to complete Manning's account of last week's meeting.

The new guests' faces showed their complete disbelief at the story of a Time Traveler.

"Time Traveler?" said Clark. "Did you see that dust on him? Could someone get that way by exploring a scientific theory?"

Filby Notices Tattered, Blood-Stained Socks!

Brice, the writer, joined in laughingly. "Aren't there any clothes brushes in the future?"

"And now for an exclusive, eye-witness report from our Special Correspondent in The Day After Tomorrow!" announced Clark, the editor, and he made a trumpet sound.

Just about everybody began to laugh hysterically at the wild idea.

At this point, the Time Traveler returned, dressed in ordinary clothes. Of the change that had so startled his guests earlier, nothing remained but his haggard look.

"Listen," said Clark hilariously, "these fellows say you've been traveling into the middle of next week! How about telling us about your adventures?"

The Time Traveler sat down silently and smiled in his old way. "Where's my mutton?" he asked finally.

"What about your story?" asked Brice.

"Story be damned!" said the Time Traveler.

Trumpeting an Eye-Witness Report

"I want something to eat! I won't say a word until I get some peptone into my arteries."

"Just one word," begged Filby. "Have you been Time Traveling?"

"Yes," he answered with his mouth full.

The rest of the dinner was extremely uncomfortable. No one said anything until the Time Traveler finally pushed his plate away.

"I guess I should apologize," he said. "I was simply starving. I've had a most amazing time." He reached for a cigar and cut the end. "Let's go into the smoking-room. It's too long a story to tell over greasy plates."

He rang the bell for the servants to start clearing the table, then led the way to the adjoining room.

"Did you tell *them* about my machine?" he asked Filby, indicating the new guests.

Filby nodded. "I tried to."

"But such a thing is an impossibility!" cried Clark.

Ready To Begin His Story

"I can't argue tonight," said the Time Traveler. "I don't mind telling you the story, but I'm in no shape to argue. I'll tell you what happened to me, but please, no interruptions."

No one spoke.

"I was in my lab this afternoon at four o'clock. Since then, I've lived eight such days as no human being has ever lived before."

"Eight days in one? How can that be?" asked Brice.

"Look, I deeply want to tell the story, even though I know most of it will sound like I'm lying. But it's true, every word of it. Is it agreed that there will be no interruptions?"

"Agreed," echoed the guests.

The Time Traveler settled back in his chair like a weary, old man. The circle of light from a little lamp shone on his white, sincere face, and his voice was filled with emotion as he began to speak.

"Please, No Interruptions."

His Story in His Very Own Words

CHAPTER 4

Landing in the Year 802,701 A.D.

Most of the listeners were in the shadow, for the candles in the smoking-room had not been lit. The small lamp shone on only the speaker's earnest face, on the writer's puzzled face, and on the lower legs of the portly editor.

As the Time Traveler began talking, the men glanced at each other every now and then. After a while, though, they stopped doing that and looked only at the Time Traveler's face. This, then, is his story, in these, his very own words:

I felt like a man about to commit suicide as

I got ready to test my machine. It was ten o'clock this very morning, right down the hall in my lab. I gave the machine one last tap, tried all the screws again, and put one more drop of oil on the quartz rod. Then I seated myself in the saddle.

"Steady," I told myself. "This is it!"

I took the starting lever in one hand and the stopping lever in the other. Then I pulled over the first and, almost immediately, the second. I felt myself trembling, and then came that feeling of falling . . . falling . . . falling you get in a nightmare. That was all. How long it lasted I didn't know.

"What's this?" I exclaimed to myself, coming awake. "Everything in the lab looks exactly the same as before. Hasn't anything happened?"

It was then that I noticed the clock. Just a moment before, it had stood at a minute or so past ten; now it was nearly three-thirty.

"This Is It!"

"It's a success! It's a success!" I told myself. "The machine has moved me through the fourth dimension — time!"

I took a deep breath, set my teeth, and this time gripped the starting lever with both hands. The lab got hazy and went dark.

I pulled the lever to its extreme position. Night came, and in another moment, morning. The lab grew fainter and hazier.

The next night came in very black, then day again, night again, day again, faster and faster each time. I had the sensation of a helpless and confused headlong movement as the lab seemed to drop away from me.

I figured the lab eventually had fallen apart along with my house, and I was now out in the open air, in the spot where the house used to be. Night continued to follow day, like the quick flapping of a black wing.

Then I saw the sun hopping swiftly across the sky, leaping it every minute.

"It's a Success! It's a Success!"

"How fast I'm traveling!" I thought. "And every minute is marking a day."

The twinkling succession of darkness and light was very painful to my eyes. I saw the moon spinning through its quarters from new moon to full moon, and I had a faint glimpse of the circling stars.

"It's amazing that I haven't moved at all through *space*," I kept telling myself. Actually, I was still on the hillside on which this house now stands. It was *time* traveling that turned night and day into continuous grayness, and made the jerking sun a streak of fire and the moon a faint wavy band.

I saw trees growing and changing like puffs of smoke — greening, browning, spreading, shivering, and passing away. I saw buildings rise up, faint and fair, then pass like dreams.

The hands of my speedometer went ever faster. The sun went up and down, up and down with such fantastic speed that I knew I

The Moon Spins Through Its Quarters.

was traveling at over a year a minute.

1900 A.D. . . . 2000 A.D. . . . 10,000 A.D. . . . 50,000 A.D. . . .

At first, I hardly thought of stopping. Then all kinds of thoughts went through my head.

100,000 A.D. . . . 200,000 A.D. . . . 500,000 A.D. . . .

"I wonder what's happened to the human race. What marvelous new advances on our simple civilization will I find?"

Next, I began to worry that something terrible would happen when I landed.

"What if some new building or other object now stands in the spot my lab used to occupy? Mightn't there be a collision that could blow both me and my machine into the Great Unknown?"

Finally, I had enough of wondering, of worrying and of the falling feeling. In a mood of nervous impatience, I hit the stop lever hard.

50,000 A.D.

The date dial stood at 802,701 A.D. as the machine went tumbling over and over on its side. To the loud sound of thunder, I was flung out into the air.

I think I was stunned for a moment. I found myself sprawled on a grassy lawn in front of the overturned craft. Hail was coming down around me, and it drove about the ground like smoke. Soon I was completely soaked.

All I could see through the hazy downpour were clusters of purple rhododendron bushes and a huge white marble figure.

"That's a pretty tall statue," I thought, "judging by the birch tree next to it. The tree reaches up only to the statue's shoulder."

The statue looked like a sphinx with hovering wings. Its sightless eyes seemed to be watching me; there was a faint shadow of a smile on its lips. The pedestal on which it stood was made of bronze, and it had turned green with age.

Tumbled Out in 802,701 A.D.

New worries hit my mind.

"How has man developed? Has he become cruel and insensitive? What if I seem to them like some old-world savage? What if they think of me as an animal, a foul creature to be killed?"

As the hail cleared and a blue summer sky appeared, I began to see other vast shapes — huge buildings with tall columns. Panic came over me.

"I've got to straighten you out and get out of here," I hissed to my machine.

Grappling fiercely with it, wrist and knee, I finally got it upright again, but it struck my chin hard in the process and left a deep cut. I was about to mount and take off when my courage came back.

I looked around more curiously and less fearfully at this world of the future. High on a wall of the nearest building was a round opening. Inside the opening, several figures

Looking Around Curiously

dressed in rich soft robes were watching me. Then I heard voices coming from another direction, and saw some men running from the bushes by the White Sphinx. One of these men took a pathway leading straight to the little lawn on which I stood with my machine.

He was only about four feet tall, and was dressed in a purple tunic and leather sandals. His soft, blonde hair curled around his face. He struck me as being beautiful and graceful, but delicate. His flushed face made me think of illness, rather than of health.

"This creature is no threat to me," I said, my confidence now returning.

The young man came right up to me without any fear and laughed into my eyes. Then he turned and spoke in a very strange, but sweet-sounding language to the two who were following him. They, too, laughed.

I let them come closer and touch my hand. Then they ran their little pink hands over my

Graceful, Delicate Creatures

back and shoulders. They seemed to want to make sure that the giant they faced was real.

But when they began to touch the Time Machine, I made a warning gesture. "Uh-uh," I said, "off limits. That's my return ticket from your playland."

That reminded me of a danger I had forgotten all about. The Time Machine must not be operated by anyone else while I was away from it. "Better not take any chances," I told myself.

I reached over the bars of the machine, and unscrewed the little levers that would get it started. These I put safely in my pocket.

Removing the Starting Levers

Large Eyes, with a Dull Look to Them

CHAPTER 5

Strange Little People

Now that I had a chance for a closer look at these future men, I noted some strange qualities. They all had curly hair that ended sharply at the neck and cheek. Their china-like faces had no trace of hair. They had unusually small ears, pointy chins, and tiny mouths with thinnish red lips. As for their eyes, they were large, with a dull look to them, as if they were not much interested in the world around them.

They just stood there, smiling, speaking softly, and cooing to each other. Clearly, it was up to me to start the conversation, if we were going to communicate at all.

I thought I would begin by pointing to my craft. "Time Machine," I said.

Then I touched my chest. "I came in machine."

There was no response so far. To express the idea of time (the way I had traveled), I pointed to the sun.

"Sun," I said. "You know, planets go round and round. Make days, months, years."

Silence. Then one of the little purple-clad creatures stepped forward. He, too, pointed skyward, but still did not speak.

"802,701 A.D.," I thought. "Man must have become very bright. Maybe he's reading my mind and instantly translating my language."

I could hardly wait to hear what he would say. "What brilliant evidence of wisdom in art, science, or the universe will his comments reveal?" I wondered.

To my intense disappointment, all he did

Pointing to the Sun

was point to the sun, and go "Blahmm!" in imitation of a thunderclap.

Good Lord! His response showed me that he had the mentality of one of our five-year-old children. He wanted to know if I had come from the sun in a thunderstorm!

For a moment, I felt I'd built the Time Machine for nothing. "So this is future man," I thought. "Light-limbed, fragile-faced, and baby-brained!"

I nodded, pointed to the sun, and made a loud thunder sound. "BLA-A-HMM!"

Startled, they drew back a few steps and bowed. Then one laughing man came back, carrying a chain of beautiful flowers. He put it around my neck as the others cooed and applauded.

Then they all began to run to and fro for flowers, and laughingly flung them at me until I was almost smothered in the most fantastic blossoms I had ever seen. These delicate, col-

A Chain of Beautiful Flowers

orful blooms were obviously the result of many centuries of culture. I stared in wonder at the blue-green puffs, the rosy-orange clusters, and the gold-fringed ruffles. Their aroma was like a shop counter of perfume bottles suddenly uncapped.

Then one of them must have decided that I should be exhibited to all their people, so they led me gently past the White Sphinx to a vast gray building of ridged stone.

Crowds of these little people were gathering by the enormous doors which opened before me, shadowy and mysterious.

The arch of the doorway, I noted as I passed through, had ancient carvings on it. These carvings were badly broken and weather-worn.

"Looks like this place has seen better days," I said.

The big doorway opened into a great hall, whose roof was in shadows. Its windows were partly coated with colored glass and partly

Ancient Carvings on the Doorway Arch

uncoated — an effect which let in a softened light. The floor was made up of huge blocks of very hard white metal.

"Plenty of footsteps, whole generations of them, must have worn these tracks," I thought, looking at the most often-used routes.

Long, low tables made of polished stone slabs and raised about a foot off the floor filled the hall. An abundance of cushions were scattered about, and the little ones who had brought me here promptly plumped themselves down on them. They motioned for me to do likewise, and I did so.

I looked around the hall slowly and was amazed by its broken-down appearance. The stained-glass windows were cracked in many places, the curtains on their lower end were thick with dust, and corners of the marble tables were chipped.

Without any ceremony, the little people

An Invitation to Sit Down

reached for the fruits heaped on the tables. They began to eat them with their hands, flinging peels and pits into the round openings on the sides of the tables.

"Looks like every day's a picnic here," I said. "Well, I'm both hungry and thirsty, so count me in, and thank you."

Except for some rather overdried raspberries and oranges, the fruit was all completely new to me. However, after tasting a blue cottony blob, a purplish wire, and little green hearts, I found them to be juicy and filling.

"Say, this tastes good," I said as I held up a flowery beige thing in a three-sided shell. "What do you call it?"

They just giggled and went on eating.

I found out later that fruit was the only food they ate. "They must be vegetarians," I reasoned, "because horses, cattle, sheep, dogs, birds, and fish had probably become extinct."

Eating with Their Hands

I decided the next thing for me to do was learn their language. This proved to be a harder job than I had expected.

Holding up one of the fruit, I asked again, "What do you call this?"

My question was met with blank stares.

I picked up another fruit, pointed to it, and said again, "What's your word for this?"

I even raised my eyebrows in a questioning expression. Again, nothing but stares and laughter.

Finally, one fair-haired creature caught on and murmured, *"Glinna."*

"Glinna," I quickly repeated.

They began to chatter and explain the business at great length to each other.

"Glinna, glinna, glinna," went down the line, with a lot of giggling and pointing.

My first attempts to imitate the little musical sounds of their language brought on peals of laughter. It was a strange situation.

"What Do You Call This?"

Here I was, trying to learn from them, but I felt like a serious schoolteacher among a class of playful children.

I persisted, though, and after some time, at least I could name a few things in their language. I had learned *arla, arna,* and even the all-important *numnee* — "this," "that," and "to eat."

But it was hard work getting them to pay attention; I had never met people who were more lazy or more easily tired. I was amazed, too, by their lack of interest. Here I was, a strange and different-looking creature dropped into their midst. Oh, they would come up to me with eager cries of surprise, all right. But then, like children bored with a new toy, they would wander away in search of some other plaything.

When I walked out of the great hall, the calm of evening was on the world, lit by the warm glow of the setting sun.

The Calm of Evening

"I should get a wider view of our planet in the year 802,701," I thought.

I therefore decided to climb to the top of a crest about a mile and a half away. Everything I passed looked so different. Even the Thames River, so close to my home in Richmond, seemed to have shifted its position a mile away.

A little way up the hill, I came upon a big granite and metal ruin — the remains of some vast structure. Amid its crumbled walls were thick heaps of beautiful, pagoda-shaped bushes, with tinted brown leaves.

"What could this building have been used for originally?" I wondered.

Although I couldn't have known it at this time, it was right here that I would soon have a very weird experience and get the first hint of an even weirder discovery — but more of that later.

A Big Granite and Metal Ruin

Struck with Odd Thoughts

CHAPTER 6

The Time Machine Vanishes

As I sat resting on the hill, it struck me as odd that there were no small houses around, only palace-like buildings. Had the single cottage, and maybe the family too, disappeared?

Looking back at the half-dozen little figures who were following me, I realized still another way in which things were different from our day.

These people all had the same girlishly rounded limbs and hairless faces, and they all wore the same silky-soft type of tunic.

Looking at them now, I couldn't distinguish the men from the women. What's more, the children seemed like slightly smaller versions of their parents.

I began to puzzle out how this similarity of the sexes had come about. It had to be because they lived a life of security and ease.

"It's only in an age of physical force," I told myself, "that men must be strong fighters and women, soft homebodies. But when there is no violence, there is no need for the family unit, so the special roles of male and female in caring for children's needs have disappeared."

These ideas sounded convincing, but before long, I was to discover how very wrong my fine-sounding conclusions were.

I pushed on to the crest of the hill, passing something that looked like a well with a cupola, or domed top, covering it.

"My, my!" I remember marveling to myself. "So that old-fashioned way of getting water

A Well with a Cupola Covering It?

has survived this long into the future."

At the top of the hill, I found a seat of a yellow metal that was unfamiliar to me. The seat was pitted with a pinkish rust and was half-smothered in moss. Each of its armrests was shaped like the head of a griffin — that mythical beast with the head and wings of an eagle, and the body and hind legs of a lion.

From here I had an excellent view. The sun had sunk below the horizon, and the western sky was a flaming gold, touched with horizontal bars of purple and red. Below was the Thames River Valley, with the river like a shiny steel band.

As my eyes traveled over the land, I saw great palaces, some in ruins and some that looked lived-in, dotting the assorted greenery. Here and there were huge white or silver statues. But there were no private homes, no hedges or fences to mark off property, and absolutely no signs of farming. The earth had

A Strange Metal Seat

become one huge, wild garden. And again I found myself wondering. "What has happened to mankind since my day? It certainly looks like it is dying out."

I reasoned that evidently man had reached some kind of peak in his accomplishments. He had managed to wipe out disease, and he had perfected plants to nourish himself easily, for I saw no weeds or bugs around.

"There's a mystery here," I told myself. "How come the little people are so well dressed, and yet I never see anybody at work? And there are no transportation vehicles or traffic, either. What about the shops and businesses and factories that played such important parts of everyday life in my time?"

While I was in this curious mood, one question led to another. "How did the people on my planet get so soft and empty-headed?"

I could only guess at the answer. "I'll bet that not having to work has ruined humanity.

One Question Leads To Another.

Man needs to struggle, to face hardships in order to be strong, energetic, and intelligent."

Then how did I explain these little people? "With no wars, animals, or disease to fight, the weak people survived better than the strong, because they weren't as restless, and they lived a life of contented idleness."

It seemed to me that even man's artistic spirit was gone. I had seen no evidence of great new paintings, murals, or sculpture. I had heard no melodious musical instruments nor ringing choruses of human voices. All that remained of the arts was seen in the little people's decorating themselves with flowers and singing and dancing in the sunlight.

What a simple explanation, and so believable too! There was only one thing the matter with it. It was completely wrong. Yes, I was soon to learn the surprising and terrible truth!

Ready to descend from the hill as the full

All That Remained of the Arts!

moon came up, I noticed that the bright little figures had stopped moving about in the valley below. I looked for the building I knew, and my eye traveled to the White Sphinx on the bronze pedestal. But something was wrong! I could see the silver birch against it and the purple rhododendrons, black now in the pale moonlight, around it. There, too, was the little lawn I had landed on. Or was it?

"No!" I cried out. "No, it cannot be the same lawn. . . " Yet the Spinx *was* facing it. But the Time Machine was gone!

"*I mustn't* be marooned in this strange world!" I thought, running down the slope, frantic with fear.

Once I fell and cut my face, but jumped up and ran on, ignoring the warm trickle of blood down my cheek and chin. I must have covered the two miles from the crest to the lawn in ten minutes.

I ran around the black tangle of

Running Down the Slope and Falling

rhododendron bushes furiously, but finally stopped, my hands clutching my hair in agony. Above me, the great White Sphinx seemed to be smiling, mocking my dismay.

"My machine!" I cried. "How has that huge machine disappeared?"

I had to stop my panic and try to think clearly. Perhaps the Eloi, as the little people were called, might have wanted to help me by moving it to a sheltered spot. But I knew very well that they had neither the brains nor the muscle power to budge the thing

"It can't have been taken on another time trip," I told myself, "for I have the stop and start levers right here with me."

I fingered them in my pocket nervously as I faced up to the frightening fact that some other power I hadn't yet met up with had taken my invention.

I must have hit the edge of madness then. I remember running in and out of the bushes

"My Machine!"

around the Sphinx, yelling, "Where is it? Where can it be?"

I remember startling some white animal, which, in the dim light, I took for a small deer. Then, sobbing and raving, I headed for the great stone building.

The big hall was dark, silent, and deserted. I slipped on the uneven floor and fell over one of the marble tables, almost breaking my shin. I lit a match and went into a second great hall, where about twenty of the little people were sleeping on cushions.

"Where is my Time Machine?" I bawled, grabbing them and shaking them. What a dumb thing for me to do!

Some of the little people laughed, and others looked frightened. This, by the way, surprised me, because I had thought man had forgotten fear in this day and age.

I ran out into the moonlight, sobbing and screaming wildly, "Lord, how could you do

"Where Is My Time Machine?"

this to me? ... Is this my fate — to be a strange animal in a world I don't know?"

I flung myself down on the ground near the White Sphinx, crying continuously until I finally fell asleep.

I awoke in a different mood. In the freshness of the morning, I still felt sad, but I was calmer now, thinking more clearly and determined to try to make some plans.

Maybe if I had to, I could eventually find the materials to build another Time Machine. But before I attempted that, I had to be certain that it hadn't been taken and hidden. If that were so, I had to find the machine's hiding place and get it back, either by force or by cunning!

Finally Falling Asleep

Peering Down a Well-Shaped Structure

CHAPTER 7

Weena of the Eloi

In my search for my missing Time Machine, I couldn't help noticing a large number of the round, well-shaped structures like the one I had seen before. I tried to peer down one of them, but couldn't see any bottom. There was, however, a dull thudding sound coming from them, as though from an engine.

"My Time Machine wouldn't be down there," I thought. "The opening is too narrow. And there's no point in questioning the Eloi any further. That's a complete waste of time, because they either don't understand my gestures, or laugh at them as if I were entertaining them at a comedy show."

Actually, investigating the ground helped me more, for on it, I saw signs of my machine being dragged. Alongside were peculiar narrow footprints, like those a sloth might make. I followed these tracks to the side of the bronze pedestal of the Sphinx, and there, I found an interesting surprise.

"The side of the pedestal has panels in it," I cried. "They're doors that open from the inside. So that's where my machine is! I must get inside. But how?"

When some of the little people passed, I signaled and called, "Say, how can I get these doors open?"

Their response startled me. These faces that always seemed only to laugh and sing were suddenly covered with expressions of horror!

I began to bang my fists on the panels. Once, I thought I heard a chuckle inside, but nothing happened.

"I Must Get Inside. But How?"

I ran to the river for a rock, then banged even harder till I flattened part of the brass covering. . . . Nothing.

"Well," I said to myself, "you won't get anywhere this way. Be calm and think sensibly. Face this world and learn its ways. Don't jump to conclusions and maybe in the end you'll find a few clues."

So I kept on trying to learn more of their language, but it was a joke — their words were as limited as their minds.

Then, I made a special friend. It happened in this way.

One day, some of the Eloi were swimming in the shallow part of the river. Suddenly, one of them ran into trouble. She seemed to have developed a cramp, and the current was carrying her downstream.

In spite of her poor little cries, nobody moved to help her. Everyone continued swimming, splashing, and frolicking in the

Nobody Moves To Help Her.

water as if she didn't exist.

"Hey, look, over there!" I shouted from the bank. "One of you, go get her!"

I couldn't believe it. There she was, about to drown right before their very eyes, and they just ignored her. What strange creatures!

"Don't cry, little one. I'll save you," I called, hoping my voice would cheer her, even though she did not understand my language.

Quickly, I slipped off my jacket and waded in at a point lower downstream. There, I was able to catch the pathetic little thing as the current was dragging her, and pulled her safely to land. I rubbed her arms and legs a bit, and she soon came round.

The truth is, I had such a low opinion of her people that I didn't expect her to express any thanks. Once again, I was wrong.

Later that day, when I came back from exploring the area, I found the little woman I had rescued waiting for me. She greeted me

Pulling the Girl Safely to Land

with cries of delight and gave me a huge garland of flowers, which apparently she had made especially for me.

I tried as best as I could to let her know I was pleased, and we sat down to "talk" to each other. At first, our conversation was mostly smiles; I thought of her as a happy child.

She told me her name was Weena, and she kissed my hands. I kissed her hands too, and decided to try to give her a lesson in English.

" Hands, " I said, holding mine up.

At first, she merely giggled. Then, out of a strongly felt urge to please me, I guess, she attempted to repeat the word.

But later, when I held her little hand and asked, *"Nootee arla?"* ("What is this?") she looked blank.

Clearly, it was up to me to learn Eloi talk. From now on, when I tell you what she said to me, you must understand that she spoke her

Weena Kisses the Time Traveler's Hands

own language, not ours.

There was a strange song that Weena and the others sang — a chant that was accompanied by a little dance. Even after I learned the meaning of the words, I still didn't understand what it was all about. I took it to be some childish nursery rhyme.

"In the light time, dance and leap,
Gather flowers, laugh and sing.

When the moon comes, danger springs,
And pulls the Eloi underground.

To the place where evil dwells,
From that darkness, none return.

Many a time as I watched Weena go through the actions of the song, I smiled, completely unaware of its grim message.

As time passed, I had mixed feelings about my friendship with Weena. True, I had been lonely, and it was nice to have someone take a

Weena's Strange Song and Dance

special interest in me. But she was so child-like, always following me around during my explorations, falling back exhausted, and then calling after me and crying when I continued on alone.

I'm afraid I didn't realize how much she meant to me, at first. She seemed to grow on me, though, until the point where returning to the White Sphinx area was almost like coming home. I began to look for her tiny white and gold figure as I came over the hill.

From Weena, I learned that fear had *not* left the world. Although she was at ease in the daylight, she dreaded the night, with its shadows and darkness. This and the song set me to thinking and observing.

I noticed that the little people always gathered into the great houses after dark and slept in crowds. If I ever entered at night without a light, it threw them into a panic. I never found an Eloi outdoors once darkness

Gathering in a Great House After Dark

fell, nor sleeping alone indoors at night.

But I was still such a blockhead that I totally missed the *reason* for their fear.

Even though it troubled Weena a lot, I insisted on sleeping away from all the crowds. Her affection for me won out over her fears, and for all the five nights that I knew her, she slept with her head pillowed on my arm.

My meeting with Weena soon blocked from my mind a horrible dream I had had the night before I met her — the night I had cried myself to sleep. Still, every so often, the nightmare came back into my thoughts.

I remember how I had cried out, "Help, help, I'm drowning! Now I'm at the bottom of the sea. Ugh, what are these horrible sea-plants brushing all over my face? Help!"

I had awakened, startled, with the odd impression that some grayish animal had just rushed out of the hall. I was confused about what was the dream and what was reality.

A Nightmare

I left the great hall in that eerie time between dying moonlight and pale dawn. As I looked up the hill, I thought I saw some white, ape-like creatures running about. One of them seemed to be carrying a body. But as the sky grew brighter, I didn't see them anymore.

"They must have been ghosts," I joked to myself. " I wonder when they lived."

How could I have been such a blind fool!

Then the next day, I rescued Weena, and all impressions of ghosts and white animals were driven from my mind.

On my fourth morning in 802,701 A.D., I was looking for shelter from the blazing sun and thinking how much hotter it was than in our time. In a colossal ruin near the great hall where I slept and ate, I found a dark, shaded area and entered it, groping along the fallen masses of stone.

Suddenly, I stopped, spellbound. A pair of shiny eyes was watching me in the darkness.

Seeing Ghosts

"What Are You, Anyway?"

CHAPTER 8

Down to the "Bad Place"

I was afraid to turn. Clenching my hands, I stared back into the glaring eyeballs. Suddenly, I remembered the Elois' strange terror of the dark, but I refused to let it overpower me. I conquered my fear a bit and stepped forward.

"What are you, anyway?" I said harshly.

I put out my hand and touched something soft. The eyes shifted, and a white shape ran past me.

With my heart in my mouth, I turned to see a weird little apelike figure, its head held down peculiarly as it ran across the sunlit space behind me. It stumbled against a stone block, and in a minute was hidden in a black shadow under another ruin.

It went too fast for me to see the creature clearly, but I knew its body was dull white and hairy, and it had strange, large, gray-red eyes. I couldn't tell if it moved on all fours, or ran with its forearms held low.

I followed it out into the open field, and at first I thought it had given me the slip. But when I reached one of those well-like openings I had seen earlier, I wondered if it could have slipped under the dome and disappeared down the shaft.

I leaned over the top of the well and lit a match. The small, white creature was staring up at me as it retreated down the shaft. The creature gave me the shivers, because it looked so much like a human spider. As it clambered down the wall, I became aware of a

A Stare from the Small, White Creature

series of metal foot- and hand-rests that formed a kind of ladder down the shaft.

Then my match went out. By the time I lit another, the thing had vanished. Little by little, the terrible truth dawned on me.

"Now I understand," I thought. "Man has *not* remained one species, but has branched into two distinct animals. My delicate child-people of the upper world are not the only descendants of my generation; this horrible, white underground monster that flashed before me is also my descendant."

Troublesome riddles filled my mind. These underground beasts, who I later found out were called Morlocks, had probably taken my machine. But why? And since, as I believed, the Eloi were their masters, why hadn't they made the Morlocks give it back?

I decided to confront my little friend with my questions.

"Weena dear," I asked, "there is something

A Terrible Truth Dawns.

I wish to know."

"Ask, then, oh my Life-giver," she replied in the Eloi language.

"See this grass?" I said, pointing.

She smiled and said, "Pretty grass grows green."

I pulled up a clump. "And underneath the grass is soil, right?"

She looked a bit nervous, but brought herself to say, "Soil to feed the grass and flowers."

"And now, Weena, you must tell me, what is below the soil down there?" I said firmly, as I pointed to the hole where the clump had been.

Weena's eyes shut tightly, and her little body shivered. She looked about to faint.

"Weena!" I shook her gently.

Her eyes fluttered as she seemed to recall my last question. Then, bursting into tears, she clutched at my arms as though for protection. Those, by the way, were the only

"What Is Below the Soil Down There?"

tears I ever saw in that future world.

"It's okay, Weena," I soothed. "I won't bring up the subject again."

She continued to look distressed. I had to think of something to change her mood. "Look, Weena, look. See the bright light!" I said gaily as I lit a match.

I struck one match after another, until she was smiling and clapping her hands again. She trotted along then, as I resumed my exploration of the area.

Late in the day, we passed one building which, I decided, I'd have to explore later. This bluish-green structure with an Oriental look was larger than any of the palaces or ruins I had yet seen. I would have checked it out right then and there, but something else was nagging at me — something I was trying to convince myself to do.

"You must do it," I kept telling myself.

But another voice within me kept fighting

Changing Weena's Mood

the idea, protesting, "Ugh! Those Morlocks are disgusting!"

"You've *still* got to check one of those shafts," I told myself.

"But their touch is so filthy-cold!" said my other voice.

"All the same, you'd better do it now. Soon the moon will be going through its last quarter. With the sky darkened, there'll only be *more* of those creatures around."

Little Weena danced beside me to the well, but when she saw me lean over the opening, she let out a pitiful cry.

"No, no! Not to look down there!"

"Who's looking? I'm counting on *climbing* down there."

"No! Forbidden to put hand in shaft. Shaft grows from *The Bad Place*!" she cried, pulling me away.

"I've got to find my machine. Don't be so worried. Good-bye for now, little Weena."

"Not To Look Down There!"

I kissed her and turned, but she continued to pull at me with her little hands.

Shaking her off, I looked down the shaft. I would be going down about two hundred yards by means of narrow metal bars, intended for smaller and lighter creatures than myself.

I tossed my legs over the side and began my descent. Midway down, one of the metal bars broke under my weight, almost swinging me off into the blackness beneath.

Painfully, I clung by one hand to the bar above, and I knew I had to move fast so it wouldn't happen again. I looked up briefly and saw a tiny dark blue circle of the night sky, with a star in it. Weena's head looking over the edge was no more than a small, black bump.

Clinging by One Hand to the Bar Above

"Three White Creatures Bend over Me."

CHAPTER 9

A Terrible Truth!

At last, I reached the bottom and found a narrow tunnel in the wall. Full of painful aches, I curled up to rest.

I don't know how long I lay there before I was startled by a soft hand touching my face. Quickly striking a match, I saw three of the white creatures bending over me.

The sudden brightness sent them off. They didn't seem to be afraid of me, but the light terrified them. They reminded me of fish that live in underwater darkness, whose pupils, too, are abnormally large and sensitive, and reflect light. Now, from dark gutters and tunnels, the

Morlocks' eyes were glaring at me in the strangest way.

I tried talking to them, but found their language completely different from the Elois'.

"Face it," I told myself. "You're in this alone, and you'd better start moving."

Feeling my way around the tunnel, I heard the noise of an engine running some kind of machinery. As I walked along, the noise grew louder. When I reached a large, open space, I struck another match and discovered myself in a vast arched cavern.

I have only a hazy impression of what I glimpsed before the match went out. Ghostly Morlocks were lurking about blobs of huge machinery, and a sort of white table with some kind of meal on it — *a rather large animal* — stood in the center. I wondered what large animal had survived in this world to furnish the red meat I saw.

The place was stuffy. What little air there

Huge Machinery and a Meal Table

was in this open space had the smell of fresh blood.

"Fool!" I thought to myself. "How could you have come on a trip like this with no weapons, no food, and no medicine?"

And if only I had thought to bring a camera, I would have been able to take quick shots and study them later on at my leisure.

Here I stood, like an idiot, with none of those basics and only four matches left. I had wasted half the box in showing off to the little people in the Upper-world.

Suddenly, a hand touched mine, and cold fingers brushed my face. The unpleasant smell of the Morlocks and the sound of their breathing told me there was a crowd of them around. Soon I felt the box of matches being gently pulled from my hand, and other hands began plucking at my clothing.

"Let go, you fiendish things! Get away, get away now!"

My shouting made them draw back briefly,

"Let Go, You Fiendish Things!"

but then they approached me again, more boldly than before, and their whispering and queer laughing noises frightened me horribly.

I struck another match, hoping its glare would help me escape. Luckily, I was able to stretch the life of the flame with a scrap of paper I found in my pocket, and I made my way to the tunnel before the burning paper went out.

In the blackness, I could hear the Morlock pattering after me. Soon I was being clutched by several clammy hands trying to haul me back. I lit another match and waved it in the dazzled faces. How nauseatingly inhuman they looked, with their pale, chinless faces and big, lidless, pinkish-gray eyes!

I kept moving and had to strike my third match to reach the opening of the shaft. As I groped for the projecting bars, my feet were grabbed from behind, and I felt myself being tugged violently backward.

Being Tugged Violently Backward

Desperately, I lit my last match, and in the brief second before it went out, my hand had reached the climbing bar.

Kicking with all my might, I freed myself from the grasp of the Morlocks and began to clamber speedily up the shaft, leaving the ape-like creatures peering up at me.

The climb seemed endless, and with only about twenty feet to go, I began to feel dizzy.

"Oh, no!" I prayed. "Please don't let me pass out now."

I really had to struggle to keep my hold on the bars and not faint. My head swam, and I felt a falling sensation a few times. Finally, after what seemed like forever, I climbed over the mouth of the well and staggered into the blinding sunlight.

I fell upon my face. Even the soil smelled sweet and clean. I remember a faraway feeling that Weena was kissing my hands, and a dim impression that other Eloi voices were nearby.

Reaching the Sweet, Clean Soil

Then I blacked out.

When I came to, Weena was chanting to herself, "Bad times, bad times, bad times coming."

"What do you mean?" I asked. "What bad times?"

"Old moon go away. Old moon leave us."

"But there'll be a new moon, little worrier."

"New moon no good. New moon *never* good for Eloi."

"Weena, what *are* you so upset about?"

She shuddered. *"Dark nights!"* she whispered.

She seemed so disturbed, I didn't continue the conversation further. I guessed, though, that the sickening Morlocks were at the bottom of her fear, and wondered what evil acts they did under the new moon.

Those Morlocks! I was their enemy now, too, and I had to think how to protect myself against them.

Listening to Weena's Fears

Clearly, I needed a good weapon and a safe place to sleep. All the buildings and trees I had checked in my wanderings seemed easily reachable by the Morlocks. I knew too well what great climbers they were.

Then the tall spires of the Palace of Green Porcelain — as I called the Oriental-looking building — and the gleam of its polished walls came back to my memory.

That afternoon, taking Weena upon my shoulders like a small child, I headed up the hills southwest for that building. After a while, Weena asked to get down, and she ran along beside me.

"Take pretty flowers," she said, stopping every now and then to pick them. "Weena putting them in special flower place now."

I had to smile. Weena had always puzzled over those strange places in my clothing, the pockets. Finally, in a sudden flash of insight she knew their purpose. Pockets were a funny

Weena Discovers a Use for Pockets.

kind of vase, of course. And that's where she placed the flowers at this point . . . .

. . . Here, the Time Traveler broke off his story and addressed the guests in his smokingroom directly. "In changing my jacket a while ago, I reached into my pocket and found *these*."

He put his hand into his pocket and silently placed two large, withered white flowers on the table. He stared at them thoughtfully a while.

The anxious guests all remembered their promise not to interrupt, so they waited patiently until he continued . . . .

. . . Instead of the green jade building being eight miles away, as I had estimated, it was more like eighteen miles away. In addition, the heel of one of my shoes was loose, and a nail was working its way into the sole of the other. This, combined with a swollen ankle, forced

Two Large, Withered, White Flowers

me to discard my shoes and walk in my socks.

We ate some fruit we found growing along our way and continued walking towards the Palace of Green Porcelain. We rested for a time as night came on, and as I was guarding the sleeping Weena from the Under-grounders, my thoughts turned to the people in this future world. Then suddenly... the terrible truth about the Morlocks and the Eloi hit me.

"Oh, no!" I thought. "It's too horrible to believe. Yet it all fits together, like pieces in a puzzle — the Morlocks tending machinery underground, the Morlocks supplying the Eloi with clothes and food, the Eloi's fear of the Morlocks and of darkness.... And that slaughtered animal I'd seen on the table in the cavern."

It could mean only one thing — the Morlocks raised the Eloi like cattle... and used them for their *food supply*! The Morlocks were cannibals!

The Terrible Truth Hits!

Reasoning Out a Course of Action

CHAPTER 10

Trapped by the Morlocks

At that time, I had only vague ideas about what course of action to take. But, as I lay awake that night, I calmly reasoned out my most urgent needs.

"First, I must find a strong weapon," I told myself. "Then a secure place of refuge. And next, I have to find some means of making a torch to use against the Morlocks. Also, I'll need to make some kind of battering-ram to break open the bronze doors of the White Sphinx."

I was sure that if I could rush in through

those doors, carrying a blaze of light, I could find the Time Machine and escape from this horrible place with Weena. I had made up my mind to take her back to our own time. Though she wasn't clear in her understanding of where it would be, she was quite eager to go back to my home with me.

We continued on our way to the Palace of Green Porcelain in the morning, and reached it about noon. We found it deserted and in ruins.

Ragged traces of glass hung in its windows, and large sheets of the green facing had fallen away from the rotted metal framework of the building.

Inside, instead of the usual large hall as in the other buildings, I found a long gallery lit with many side windows. The tile floor was thick with gray dust. Then I noticed several parts of huge skeletons scattered in the center of the room. They seemed to be of some long extinct creatures from prehistoric times — a

The Ruined Palace of Green Porcelain

Brontosaurus and a Megatherium.

"Of course!" I cried. "We're in an ancient *museum,* and this is the fossil room!"

Along the sides of the gallery were shelves holding glass cases of our own time. They must have been sealed to make them airtight for the fossils inside them had been fairly well preserved. I figured that the absence of bacteria and fungi in this future world had slowed down the decay of these fossils quite a bit.

Exploring further, we came to a small mineral gallery, and then to an area where huge hulks of machines were displayed. Most had rusted and broken down, but some were still in fairly good shape. But I could make only vague guesses as to what they were used for.

While I was wondering how I could use these old machines against our enemies Weena suddenly came up close to me, tugged

The Fossil Room of an Ancient Museum

at my sleeve, then took my hand.

"What's the matter, Weena?" I asked. "You look troubled."

I had been so wrapped up in the machines that I hadn't noticed the gradual lessening of light or the sloping of the gallery floor. But Weena's fears drew my attention to the fact that the gallery ran down into a thick darkness. The floor at that end had a number of small, narrow footprints. In the remote blackness, I heard a peculiar pattering and the same odd engine noises I had heard down the well.

I realized that I still didn't have a weapon to protect us, but I would need one immediately. My eyes traveled over the machines and landed on a huge lever projecting from one of them. Clambering onto the stand and grasping the lever in both my hands, I put all my weight upon it. After a minute's strain, it snapped and I rejoined Weena, now armed with a club-like

A Huge Lever for a Weapon

weapon in my hands.

"Oh, how I'd love to crack some Morlock skulls with my new club!" I said, feeling no hesitation about killing my own descendants.

Only concern for leaving Weena and my desire to find my Time Machine kept me from heading straight into that blackness and killing the Morlocks.

We passed through a section of the museum with some book tatters, then up a broad staircase into a really hopeful place — a gallery of chemistry!

The gallery was well preserved, and in one of the airtight cases, I found a box of matches. Eagerly, I tried them. They were perfectly good, not even damp from age. I was so happy I whistled a little tune and whirled about the room in a dance, as Weena watched in wonderment.

"And that, Miss 802,701, is how we dance in *my* day," I gaily cried when I was done.

Finding Perfectly Good Matches!

Then I made another find — a chunk of camphor in a sealed jar. I was just about to throw it away when I remembered something.

"Camphor can burn!" I cried. "This will make a great candle!" And I put the chunk in my pocket along with the matches.

It was frustrating next to find a great many guns, pistols, and rifles, but no bullets or gunpowder. Then, in another airtight case, I found two sticks of dynamite.

"Eureka!" I shouted and smashed the case with joy.

Taking one stick into a little side gallery, I tested it out. I waited five minutes . . . ten . . . fifteen for an explosion, but it never came. They were dummies.

"Too bad!" I told Weena. "I might have used them to blow up the doors of the Sphinx to get my Time Machine. But maybe I can force those doors open with my wonderful iron club."

Two Sticks of Dynamite

My plan now was to head for the White Sphinx, getting as far as we could, now that night was approaching. I was no longer afraid of sleeping in the open, knowing I had matches and camphor, and could build a fire to keep the Morlocks away.

As we walked, I stopped to pick up a stick and dried grass. With these loaded in my arms, our progress was slowed. When we reached the edge of the forest, which I took to be a mile across, I felt sleep coming on. But then with the darkness, so were the Morlocks coming on. When we stopped among the black bushes, I spotted three of them behind us.

"The best thing to do," I said, "is push on through the forest to the bare hillside, because that should make a safer resting place. The matches and camphor will light our path."

I realized that I couldn't deal with both striking matches and carrying firewood at the same time, so I put the wood down. And then

Three Morlocks Follow Close Behind.

— oh then it was — that I stupidly lit a fire, hoping it would startle our pursuers and cover our retreat.

Weena was fascinated by the flames dancing up from my pile of wood. This was the first fire she had ever seen, aside from the match flares. She wanted to run and play with it, and even jump in it, but I picked her up bodily and plunged ahead into the woods. The glare of the fire lit our way pretty well.

Soon, I began to hear the pattering of feet behind me. I couldn't strike a match because I had Weena on my left arm and my iron bar in my right hand. Voices like those I had heard in the Under-world were closing in behind us. Then, in another minute, I felt a tug at my coat, followed by one at my arm.

Weena shuddered violently, then was still. I had to put her down to light a match. As I fumbled in my pocket, a struggle began in the darkness about my knees, with Weena silent

Carrying Weena Away from the Fire

and the Morlocks making peculiar cooing sounds.

The spurt of light from my match showed Weena clutching at my feet, her face to the ground.

"Weena, Weena! " I cried, bending to her.

She was barely breathing. I lit the camphor block and flung it to the ground, where it split and flared up. This temporarily drove the Morlocks back to the shadows, and I knelt down and lifted up my unconscious little friend.

The woods behind us seemed full of the stir and murmur of a big crowd!

"Weena, Weena!"

Lost in the Forest

CHAPTER 11

The Time Machine Is Found

I put the unconscious Weena on my shoulders and was about to dash on when a horrible realization hit me! These last few minutes, what with stopping to light a match and kneeling to tend to Weena, I had turned myself about a few times. Now, I had no idea of the right direction for getting out of the forest and no idea how close the Morlocks were to us. I broke out in a cold sweat.

"I'd better build a fire," I told myself, "because now we'll have to camp where we are until dawn."

I put Weena down on the soft grass and began collecting sticks and leaves. Then I lit a match, and in its light, I saw two white forms reaching for the unconscious Weena.

One of the Morlocks was so blinded by the light that as he tried to escape, he ran straight into me. I swung instinctively, and the crunching of his bones sounded good under my fist.

Then I noticed that the branches above me were quite dry. This was not surprising, since it hadn't rained at all since my arrival a week ago. I broke off several of these branches and soon had a smoky fire of green wood and dry sticks. With this, I was able to save my camphor.

"Weena, poor little Weena," I murmured as I tried to revive her. But she lay as one dead. I wasn't even sure that she was breathing.

I was exhausted, and the smoke from the fire was making me drowsy. I caught myself

Swinging at a Morlock

nodding as I began to doze. Then, with a start, I opened my eyes to an awful change.

It was completely dark, and the Morlocks had their hands on me. I shoved their fingers off and felt for the box of matches. But it was gone!

Then I understood what had happened. I had fallen asleep, and my fire had gone out. What an unspeakable sensation to have those horrible fingers clawing at my neck, my hair, my arms. It was like being in a monstrous spider web. I felt my death very near.

Under the weight of the hideous pack, I went down. Little teeth were nipping at my neck. I rolled over, and as I did so, my hand touched my iron club. The second my fingers clutched it, I felt an instant surge of power. I swung it about wherever I thought their faces were, and joyously felt the smashing of flesh and bone as I struck. For the moment I was free.

In a Monstrous Spider Web!

That wild, excited feeling that comes with a hard fight came over me. Though I was sure both Weena and I couldn't win and that we'd wind up as a feast for the Morlocks, I was determined to make the Morlocks pay dearly for their meat. With my back against a tree, I kept swinging.

Then something unexpected happened. The Morlocks' voices grew louder and their movements grew faster, but none of the creatures came within reach.

"Hah!" I cried madly. "Come on, you fiends! Are you afraid, or have you given up?"

The darkness seemed to take on a glow, and I could suddenly see three Morlocks battered at my feet and the rest running away through the woods in front of me.

As I stood bewildered, I saw a little red spark fly between the branches, and I smelled burning wood. In an instant, I understood. The forest was aflame. The fire I had foolishly set

176

"Come On, You Fiends!"

had spread and was now coming after us.

"Weena, Weena!" I called frantically. I looked for her, but she was gone.

The hissing and crackling behind me and the explosive thud as each fresh tree burst into flame left me little time for thinking. Still gripping my iron bar, I followed the Morlocks' path.

At last I came to a small open space, away from the swift-moving flames. There, I saw the most hideous sight of any I had seen in that future world.

With a fence of flaming trees encircling the open area, thirty or forty Morlocks, blinded by the light, were blundering about, crashing into each other.

At first I didn't understand their blindness, and I kept striking furiously at them, killing one and crippling others. But when I saw one of them groping about and heard their moans of misery, I realized that in the light, they

The Morlocks are Blinded by the Light.

were helpless. And I struck at them no more.

I walked about the hill among them, looking in vain for some trace of Weena. But she was gone.

Time and again, I saw some Morlocks put their heads down in a kind of agony and rush into the flames.

"Oh, God!" I cried. "Please let me wake up from this terrible nightmare!"

But it was no dream, and it seemed like forever before the fire began to die down, and the white light of day arrived.

Once again, I searched for signs of Weena, but there were none. The Morlocks had probably left her poor little body somewhere in the forest. I was relieved that at least she didn't have to suffer the dreadful fate the cannibalistic Morlocks usually planned for any Eloi they captured.

From where I stood on the top of a hill, I could make out through the smoke the Palace

Searching for Signs of Weena

of Green Porcelain. From there, I could figure out the location of the White Sphinx.

So, leaving the remaining Morlocks still running about blindly and moaning wildly, I tied some grass around my stocking feet and limped over the smoking ashes toward where I was sure my Time Machine lay hidden.

I felt miserable. Not only was I tired and lame, but I was also terribly depressed by Weena's horrible death.

A feeling of loneliness came over me, and, with a painful longing, I began to think of this house, this fireside, and of you, my friends.

About nine in the morning, I came again to the yellow metal seat from which I had viewed the world the first evening of my arrival. How beautiful the world had seemed then! How different were my impressions now!

Slowly, I moved down the hill towards the White Sphinx. I had my iron bar in one hand, while the other fingered some loose matches I

Coming Again to the Yellow Metal Seat

had discovered in my pocket. They must have spilled out of the box before that wild scene when the Morlocks were boldly grabbing for it.

Much to my surprise, I didn't have to use my dependable iron bar on the bronze doors at all. They were completely open, having slid aside into special grooves in the wall.

I hesitated at the doors and peered inside. There, before me, on a kind of raised pedestal, stood my Time Machine!

The Bronze Doors are Completely Open.

The Bronze Doors Slide Shut.

CHAPTER 12

Escape into the Future

I stepped inside the building, and the bronze doors slid shut, as I knew they would. Those pallid creatures thought they had me trapped.

"Think yourselves so tricky, don't you, Morlocks? But don't think you have me fooled, not for one minute. I understand the way your sickly minds work."

There were three important things they didn't know. First, I'm sure they didn't understand what the Time Machine was for — that it would whisk away their intended victim forever. Second, they were unaware that I carried on me the levers that would make it go. And third, they didn't suspect I still had some matches in my possession. I was counting heavily on this last fact to surprise them.

I could already hear their hideous laughter as they came towards me. Calmly, I tried to strike a match, only to discover that I had overlooked one little thing — the matches were the kind that could be lit only by striking them on the rough side of a box. My *loose* matches were useless!

All my cool disappeared as I began hitting wildly at my attackers with the iron bar and control levers from the Time Machine.

"Oh, no, you don't!" I cried as one of the fiends grabbed a lever from my hand. I had to butt him in the skull with my own head to get it back.

Working frantically, I managed to drop the iron bar onto the floor of my Time Machine and slip the levers into place. Then I pulled the starting one over to activate the system.

Getting Back the Control Lever

The clinging hands of the Morlocks slipped from me. The darkness disappeared, and I found myself moving again in the gray light I had been in earlier.

In my rush to escape from the Morlocks, I hadn't even seated myself comfortably in the saddle. So I was now rushing through time in an awkward sideways position, clinging to the machine as it swayed and vibrated.

Suddenly, I brought myself to look at the dials, and I discovered that I had unthinkingly pulled the lever in the wrong direction — I was moving into the future, instead of going back to my day. Still I didn't change the lever.

As I drove on, a peculiar change crept over this future world. The blinking of light and dark — the change from night to day — grew slower and slower. The sun had stopped setting — it simply rose slightly in the West and dropped back in place, growing broader

Rushing Through Time Sideways

and redder. All trace of the moon had vanished, and the stars were circling slower and slower.

Finally, a steady darkness fell over the earth. Our planet was no longer spinning; it had come to rest.

Ever so carefully I began to reverse the motion of my machine, until it came to a gentle stop.

The sky was no longer blue, but rather inky black with pale white stars. On the horizon, the sun lay red and motionless.

"What will I find here now?" I wondered. "World, what are you like?"

Looking out of my machine, I saw I was on a beach. A clump of reddish rocks and some moss-green plant growth surrounded me. The sea stretched to the horizon, but there were no waves.

I was breathing very fast, because the air was thinner than it is now. From far up a

"World, What Are You Like?"

desolate slope, I heard a harsh scream and saw a creature like a huge, white butterfly go fluttering up to the sky and disappear. The sound of its voice was so dismal that I shivered and seated myself more solidly upon the machine.

Looking around again, I saw that what I had taken for a reddish clump of rocks was slowly moving toward me.

It was a monstrous crab-like creature as large as a table, its big claws swaying, its huge eyes protruding on stalks, and its long, whip-like antennae waving. Its back was ridged with a greenish crust; its ugly, sectioned mouth was flickering and feeling as the monster lumbered towards me.

Then I felt a tickling on my cheek and brushed away what I thought was a fly. Another came by my ear, and when I struck at it and caught it, I found it was the antenna of another monster crab that had come up behind

Monstrous Crabs!

me. Its evil eyes were wiggling on their stalks, and its mouth was alive with a craving appetite.

I hurriedly pulled the lever and put a month's time between myself and these monsters.

I was still on the same beach, where I saw dozens of those grotesque giant crabs crawling among the intense green plant life. The desolation that hung over the world was appalling!

I moved on a hundred years, but saw much the same sight. So I traveled on, stopping every thousand years or more, interested in finding out what eventually happened to our planet.

At last, more than thirty million years from now, the huge sun had come to take up nearly a tenth of the sky. The earth was dying. Now the beach was white, and all the crabs and plant life had disappeared. It was bitter cold

Thirty Million Years from Now

and snow kept falling along the ice-fringed sea and on the higher inland slopes.

As my gaze turned back to the sun, I noticed its outline begin to change, as if something was eating away at it. It grew darker and darker, and as blackness crept over the day, I realized what I was seeing.

"It's an eclipse," I said to myself. "Either the moon or another planet is passing between the earth and the sun."

All I was aware of was this blackness, the snow, and . . . silence.

Then the edge of the sun began to reappear. I thought I saw an object flopping about on a sandbar near the shore. Was there still life on earth?

I got off the machine and walked to the water's edge for a closer look. Yes, it *was* moving. It was a round thing about the size of a football. Tentacles trailed down from it, and it seemed black against the freezing-cold,

Is There Still Life on Earth?

blood-red water as it hopped about.

The cold, the darkness, and the thinness of the air began to get to me. I felt like fainting, but the thought of lying helpless on that deserted beach in the darkened future forced me to pull myself back on the saddle of my Time Machine.

"Hang in there," I told myself, "or you'll never get back to the world you know."

"Hang In There."

Bring Back . . . Nothing!

CHAPTER 13

The Golden Age of Science

I pulled the lever and sped homeward to my native time, thinking how sadly lacking in accomplishments my trip had been. What wondrous healing salve, what formula for peace, what marvelous new hope for my race was I bringing back to share? . . . None at all, nothing whatsoever.

"All I can show for my week of maddening strain and frantic activity are bruises, bitterness, and the memory of a tragic love."

I made up my mind, therefore, to make one more stop. But what date to choose?

THE TIME MACHINE

Three hundred years from home, I figured, I would reach the Golden Age of Science. Like Prometheus, the Greek god who brought men fire, I'd return with some dramatic new way to help my fellow man.

With my eyes ever on the dial as I hurtled back through the alternating light and darkness, I chose the proper moment and pulled the lever over. Shuddering, my Time Machine lurched to a stop.

I looked up and noticed that where a tiled ceiling had once covered my lab, there was now a high, transparent dome, with colored liquids pulsating along it in glass-like pipes.

Abruptly, a hand that was gloved in silvery silk reached in and squirted something near my face. It smelled like roses.

"How wonderful! " I thought. "In my day, in the South Seas, people always welcomed newcomers with floral wreaths. It looks like that custom has spread and lasted into the

A Silvery Hand Squirts Something.

twenty-second century. What a pleasant greet-ing!"

But my good mood began to diminish as I sensed a strange change in my body. Then that mood vanished completely when a pair of hands pulled me roughly out of the machine.

A figure in a silver cape and tights, with gloves to match, was saying, "That's enough Apathy-Gas, Kolar. There's only one passenger."

So *that* was why I felt so apathetic — why I was so unconcerned that I never thought to raise my hands in resistance. I really had no desire to do anything.

First, I let another silver-clad figure search me, then I passively allowed myself to be led to no-matter-where.

It turned out to be the Truth Room, this very smoking-room we're sitting in right now converted into a kind of interrogation office.

The first thing I noticed was four enor-

Pulled Roughly Out of the Machine

mous portraits on the wall. They were all of people in white lab-coats. In one, an Oriental woman was peering at a kind of chemical tube. In another, a black man sat by an elaborate microscope. In the third, a red-skinned woman was working with a tri-square and compass. And in the last, a white man stood in front of a blackboard covered with complicated symbols.

"Truth-Pellet, Taggett," ordered the tall, white-haired man from behind his elaborate, gadget-covered desk. This man, obviously their leader, appeared to be in his fifties, and the caped uniform he wore was dark purple. The three others in the room all wore softer shades of clothing.

The man called Taggett reached his silver-gloved fingers into a dispenser-box strapped to his middle and pressed a lever. A small, cigar-shaped capsule popped out. Taggett held it aloft and snapped it in two. "Ready, sir," he said.

Inside the Truth Room

A wispy pink cloud rose slowly to the ceiling, drifted down, and was gone.

"Now," said the one in command, "set the interpreting machine and hook him up. We'll soon find out which of their languages he speaks and change it into ours."

"You really think he's one of them?" asked a blonde, blue-caped man.

"Of course, Darton," answered the leader. "Did you ever see such garments in all of Northdom?"

"Never," said Darton.

"Never," agreed Taggett. "But do you think he may have escaped from Southdom? Look how bruised he is, and notice the condition of his clothes."

"It's an old Southdom trick to fool us," said the leader. "The Truth-Pellet and the language Interpret-X will soon reveal it. Now hook him up, Kolar," and he pointed to a man-sized machine with many knobs and dials.

"Hook Him Up."

"That won't be necessary," I said quietly. "I speak your language and am, in fact, an Englishman."

"It is good that you are familiar with our tongue," said the leader. "But what is an Englishman?"

It would be hard to say who was more stunned — the four caped figures or myself. I then told them briefly about my background and my invention.

I suppose it was the influence of the Truth-Pellet that prompted me to express my intense disappointment at what I had experienced that past week.

" I should have gone straight home in Time," I finished. "But I had hoped to find myself in an advanced world, run by intelligent men of good will. Instead, here I am, a drugged captive, waiting to be questioned and locked up. And I don't even mind. Your Apathy-gas took care of that."

"What Is an Englishman?"

The silver-haired leader looked hurt. "You misunderstand," he said. "You are not our prisoner. This is necessarily our standard practice in dealing with strangers."

"But, why?" I asked.

"Out of the need to protect ourselves," said Taggett. "We didn't recognize your Time Machine for what it is, because it is such a primitive model."

"You mean you've got them, too?" I asked in amazement.

"*Had* them," said Darton. "They have been outlawed for two hundred years."

This piece of information shocked me. "Why were they made illegal?" I asked.

"Too many of our bravest and brightest people were disappearing," said Kolar.

"Remember studying about that last trip?" asked the leader.

"Who doesn't?" said Taggett. "A craft that left with two hundred forty Time-Travelers

Learning about Other Time Machines

and came back with only one survivor."

"And the story that that one told!" finished
Kolar. "A horrendous tale of an underground
race of pale, ape-like men!"

"The Morlocks!" I shouted, then shuddered.

"Well then, you know," said the leader. "We
shall have to destroy your machine at once.
You must obey our laws as well. For here, all
are equal before the law."

Before I could say anything, Darton sprang
forward. "Wait!" he cried. "Why don't we post-
pone destruction and study his machine first?
The things of his century could hold interest
for our students of history."

"You may be right, Darton," said the leader.
"Perhaps we'll wait at least one day before
dismantling the antique."

"Are all here *really* equal before the law?" I
asked.

"Without question," said Taggett. "Observe
that we did not inject you alone with the

Darton Wants To Study the Machine.

Truth-Pellet, as we could have. It was sprayed into our common air. We've all been breathing it. You have the right to question us now, if you desire."

With the waning of the Apathy-gas, my curiosity began to return. I learned that in the twenty-first century, an important turning-point in civilization had been reached.

When our squandering of nature's resources had threatened to kill off all life on earth, four scientists — the ones whose portraits I had been staring at — took drastic action.

"The founding four met from the corners of our planet to form the *World Science Governing Board,*" said the leader reverently. "They drew up plans for budgeting our energy, unpoisoning our atmosphere, and bettering the products of the earth and ocean."

"Did they have an army?" I asked.

"They didn't need one. Conditions were so

Explaining about the Founding Four

bad that national leaders everywhere were glad to hand over all power to the *W.S.G.B.* In this way, they got rid of all the life-and-death problems they couldn't solve themselves."

"You mean the whole planet was under their rule?"

"For a time, yes. A glorious interval," said the leader dreamily. "War outlawed. Disease cured. Life extended. Harmony and good fellowship everywhere."

"How long did it last?" I asked.

"One generation. Then the children of the founding four wanted to take control, instead of holding a universal election."

"What happened then?" I asked.

"Well," continued Taggett, "two factions formed, each gathering followers. Both sides found old manuals for making guns, tanks, and bombs."

"I suppose all the new scientific knowledge was put to use," I said.

A Glorious Interval—for One Generation

"Yes," said Kolar. "One group, ours, took over the North Polar area, after melting the ice pack — and causing havoc to the world's weather conditions, by the way. We filled in an island at the North Pole, and that's been our main headquarters."

"And the other group?" I asked.

"They're at the opposite end of the earth. They brought solar heating to the world's coldest continent, and are based in Antarctica."

"How many years did that war last?"

"It's still going on. Southdom is always spying, attacking, looting, and killing," said the leader. "This lab you have reached in Richmond is one of our secret bases. That's why we assumed you were an enemy invader."

"I understand. Then maybe . . ."

Just then, a noise like sirens signaling the end of the universe began to sound.

"They're approaching!" shouted somebody.

Sirens Begin To Sound.

"Man all defense craft!" the leader shouted into a box on his desk.

In the confusion, I seized the chance to run back to the lab. I had one foot over the rim of my machine, when I suddenly felt myself being yanked back.

Darton, the man in blue, was choking me. "No, not you!" he cried. "I'm going back in time. With all my knowledge, I'll dazzle the old world. They'll *worship* me!"

"So *that's* why you didn't want my machine wrecked," I sputtered.

"Farewell, and thanks," he said, and left me lying weakly on the floor.

Desperately, I hoped the Truth-Pellet had worn off as I shouted, "You'd better let me show you where the poison gas lever is, or you'll destroy yourself! "

He believed me, of course. Any craft *he'd* have built would have contained a poison gas lever.

.

224

Yanked Back by Darton

"All right, come on," he said. "But no tricks." The gloved index-finger he pointed at me had a deadly-looking gun barrel at its tip.

"It's here on the floor," I said. And reaching down, I grasped the old iron bar I had flung there in escaping from the Morlocks.

"I don't see it," he said, his last words before the bar connected with his head.

I booted his limp form out and hurled the weapon at his skull to insure my getaway. Then quickly slipping onto the saddle, I set the machine for my own home time.

The Iron Bar Connects!

Back in a Familiar Lab

CHAPTER 14

One Story Ends and Another Begins

When the dial showed today's date, I stopped the machine and saw my familiar lab and tools just as I had left them.

I got off the Time Machine very shakily and sat down on my bench, trembling violently. Then I became calmer. My workshop was exactly as it had been as if I had been in a dream . . . . But no, *not exactly*.

My Time Machine had started from the *southeast* corner of the lab, where you all saw it earlier. But it had returned to the *northwest* corner. That shows the exact distance from the lawn to the pedestal of the White Sphinx, where the Morlocks had moved it.

Then I got up and limped down the hall. Hearing your voices at dinner, I opened the door.... The rest you know. I washed, changed my clothes, had dinner, and began to tell you the story....

...The Time Traveler took a deep breath and tried to puzzle out the expressions of the faces surrounding him. "I know this sounds incredible, and I don't blame you," he said. "I find it all hard to believe myself, and yet...."

The Time Traveler looked down at the withered white flowers on the table. As he reached down to gently touch them, he studied the half-healed scars on his knuckles. "I *did* build a Time Machine and use it.... But your expressions make me wonder.... I must go look at it."

The men followed him into the lab. There

"I *Did* Build a Time Machine and Use It . . ."

stood the Time Machine, in the *northwest* corner, exactly as the Time Traveler had said. Brown spots and smears were on the ivory, and bits of grass and moss were on its lower parts. One rail was bent crooked.

The Time Traveler nodded to himself, convinced of the truth of what he had just told his guests.

As the Time Traveler saw his guests to the door a while later, Dr. Perry looked him squarely in the face and said, "You're suffering from overwork, man. You need a good rest."

"What a pity it is that you're not a story writer!" boomed Clark, the editor. "You'd make a fortune with that gaudy tale!"

"Where did you *really* get those flowers, old boy?" asked Manning, the psychologist.

Only Filby did not mock him as he shook his friend's hand soberly and whispered a soft,

Only Filby Does Not Mock Him.

smiling "Good night."

Filby couldn't sleep all that night, and the next day he stopped by to question the Time Traveler further about his incredible story.

The Time Traveler greeted Filby in his smoking-room. A knapsack and small camera were under his arms. "I know why you came," he said warmly, "and it's awfully good of you."

"What are your plans now?" asked Filby.

"Just you sit here and read some magazines," said the Time Traveler. "I'll be back in half an hour."

"Where are you going with that knapsack and camera?" asked Filby, as he thumbed through one of the magazines.

"This time I'm going to bring back proof," said the Time Traveler as he headed for the door. "Pictures and a specimen or two. Will you wait for me?"

"Of course," said Filby, almost absent-

"This Time, I'm Going To Bring Back Proof."

mindedly.... Then the full meaning of what his friend had just said hit him, and he ran down the hall to the lab.

When he reached the doorway, Filby felt a gust of wind and saw a whirling mass of black and brass ... then the flash of a transparent figure. Suddenly, a large pane of glass in the skylight came crashing to the floor. And the room was empty. The Time Machine and the Time Traveler were gone!

Filby waited, but the Time Traveler never returned. That was three years ago. Will he ever come back? Was he so disappointed with the future that he went into the past, only to encounter cavemen or an early civilization? Or did he venture again into the future? And if so, what did he discover this time?

But, perhaps most puzzling of all to Filby — was the Time Traveler remaining wherever he was by choice? Or was he being held prisoner

Gone!

of some unknown past or future form of life?

And now, whenever Filby worries about what the future holds for mankind, he finds some comfort in two strange, white flowers that he has kept all these years, although they're brown and flat and brittle by now. For they remind him that even in wretched times, concern, gratitude, love and devotion to others can still live on in the heart of man!

Comforted by Brown and Brittle Flowers